AMISH  T

by

Sandra Becker

AMISH YOUNG ROMANCE

Prologue

"What?!"

Karen could feel the room spinning. She clutched the table to steady herself, but her ears were still ringing with the words her father had just said.

"I have decided to marry you to Mark."

No, it couldn't be! How could her father take that decision without even telling her?

But of course he could. He was her father, and she... she was just a child in his eyes. Even though she was eighteen and old enough to think for herself. And Karen had already thought of who she wanted to spend her life with.

Joshua.

Karen loved Joshua, and she knew Joshua loved her. She had to tell him immediately what had happened. She felt trapped in a nightmare, and the room was still spinning.

Chapter 1

Karen woke up to the sounds of birds chirping and the sun shining through the cloth curtains that hung over her window. It was romantic in words only though. In theory it should have been a great morning. But Karen's night hadn't been all that amazing. In fact it had been filled with a great deal of turmoil.

She sat up and patted down her tussled up hair. She'd clearly been tossing and turning in the night. Karen huffed and went over to her dresser. It was a dark brown, carved intricately by her father. It was normally an artifact of happiness for her. But today, it reminded her of her father.

She reached into one of the drawers and grabbed her brush. She put it through her hair, stretched it out as she tried to brush through. It was tough and she was afraid of breaking the hair. After a few tugs though, she got it through.

Karen cleaned herself up and prepared for the morning chores. She put on her clothes and made sure her hair was tied properly in its bun. She covered her hair with a prayer *kapp*.

Morning chores began as early as the sun rising. Judging by how things looked outside, Karen was slightly late on the uptake. But she would work quickly to get everything done in time for breakfast.

Her job was mostly to maintain the farm animals. That meant feeding the horses, chickens, and other livestock. The feeding was the easy part. It was also a good morning ritual for her to have. Karen was able to take her time and greet the animals. Feeding them wasn't too labor intensive, but today she had to move faster than usual. She wondered to herself if the animals noticed that she was in a hurry.

Once the feeding was done, Karen moved on to the grooming. The sun had just risen so the heat wasn't so bad yet. Summer was approaching very quickly though and Karen wasn't looking forward to it. While summer occasionally gave way to a festive environment and good weather, it was mostly the dry heat that played terribly with Karen's hair.

An hour later, Karen had completed her

chores. She went inside to get some breakfast. The house smelled of meats and eggs being fried in the pan. Karen took her shoes off and set them by the front door. She went into the kitchen and saw her mother Miriam. She was at the stove, cooking the delicious food Karen had smelled when she came inside.

"Good morning, mother." Karen said, giving her mother a kind smile.

Miriam returned the smile gracefully. "Good morning, dear. How are the animals today?"

Karen went over to the bucket of water and washed her hands. "They're doing well. I think everything will be ready in time for the summer harvest."

Her mother's smile brightened. "That's great! Your father will be pleased to hear that."

Karen said nothing, ignoring her mother's comment. Her mom looked over at her and sighed. "Come on, dear. You can't still be mad at him."

Karen pursed her lips. She just grabbed some of the plates and began to set the table.

"You're going to need to talk to him eventually." Miriam said in a knowing tone.

"Yes, I know." Karen eventually said. "But I don't want to be angry when we talk."

Her mother shook her head. "You're of age now. It's natural to be promised to a man of prominent stature and character. Mark is a fine man, any girl would be lucky to have him."

"Is breakfast almost ready?" Karen was starving, and desperate for a change in subject.

Her mother's eyes narrowed. She knew what Karen was doing. But she wasn't going to push it yet.

A few minutes later and everything was ready. The table was set and her mother began to set out large bowls and plates with the meats and bread on them. One large plate had eggs on it. Everything smelled perfect.

One by one the rest of the family filed in and took their seats. There were her two brothers, David and Jacob, and then her father Samuel. They were strong men, who always did their best to take care of the family.

Even though Karen was angry with her

father, she couldn't forget that he was trying to have her best interests at heart.

Despite that, she still didn't like the decision he made for her. It was common for a father to marry his daughters off. But Karen would have at least hoped that he'd taken her opinion into consideration.

Mark was a nice man. He owned a good farm and came from a good family as well. But Karen didn't know him well enough to say that she would want to marry him. Was that enough for her father? No. He knew Mark's family well enough to say she would marry him.

The whole thing made her blood boil. Not only that, but she had given her heart to another man. She left that part out of the argument because she didn't want to bring someone else into it. It wouldn't be fair to him.

So instead Karen was left with staring angrily at her father from across the table. They exchanged pleasantries and went on with the beginning of the meal. They held hands and prayed before eating. Then they dove in.

The breakfast was everything Karen wanted it to be. The rest of the family enjoyed it as well. There was talk of the summer harvest and how everyone was getting ready for it. Karen did her best to stay out of it. Not only was she too hungry, but she didn't want to speak out of turn either. It was in everyone's best interest at the moment to remain cordial.

When the meal was over, everyone had a

bit of free time to themselves before more work was to be done. This work usually had to do with setting up for the harvest or making any repairs that had to be done. That was work for the men, but for Karen and her mother, a lot of baking was involved. The larger appeal of the summer harvest involved all the treats that all the women brought.

Karen decided to use her free time to meet Joshua. He lived on the land closest to hers. It wasn't a long journey for her to walk over.

I hope he would be able to figure out what to do next.

Chapter 2

Karen saw Joshua working in the field, repairing some fence posts. He was a burly man, with wide shoulders and a fit body. He was sweating under the hot sun. Joshua must have heard her approach, because he looked up and noticed her immediately. He smiled brightly and waved her over.

Karen smiled and returned the wave. Joshua took a cloth from his pocket and wiped his forehead.

"Hello Karen." Joshua said with a smile.

Karen's smile brightened. "Hello Joshua."

"How are you?" he asked, taking a deep breath. He had clearly been working hard.

"I'm… alright." Karen said, avoiding his gaze.

"Are you sure?" Joshua looked at her closely. "You sound different today."

She shrugged. "Father and I had an argument."

Joshua raised an eyebrow. "Why, what happened?"

Karen wasn't sure if she wanted to tell Joshua about Mark or not. Telling him wasn't exactly on the top of her list. The conversation would no doubt be awkward. But telling him might also motivate a change in her father. If that were the case… then it might be worth it.

"I think you need to know." Karen said.

Joshua laid down his tools and turned full

face at Karen. "Know what?"

Karen fumbled for a minute, with nothing coming out of her mouth. "My father has decided to marry me to Mark."

Joshua blinked for a moment, the words hit him hard. "What do you mean?"

Karen shook her head. "I mean that he's decided to marry me to Mark. That's all there is to it. And I can't do anything about it."

"Does he know about us?"

"No, he doesn't."

"But, he didn't ask you? Doesn't he care about what you want?" Joshua asked.

"No, he's already made up his mind. I don't know what to do." Karen said.

Joshua sighed and rubbed his chin.

"Maybe I should go talk to him. At least then he might understand where you're coming from."

Karen shrugged. "I don't know if that'll change anything."

"Well it can't hurt, right?" Joshua asked.

Karen didn't have a good answer for that. "I suppose now. But be careful. I don't want him turning against you or anything. He likes you."

"Just not enough to marry us?" Joshua said with a small laugh. He straightened himself and started off towards Karen's farm.

"You're going now?" Karen asked, surprised.

Joshua turned back to her. "Why not? The sooner we get this over with the better."

Karen wasn't sure if she should follow

him or not. This wasn't exactly a conversation she wanted to be present for. She didn't know if she should let Joshua go on his own, trail behind him, or find something else to do in the meantime.

Karen stood there in indecision as Joshua continued on. She saw that Joshua had almost reached her home. While Karen didn't want to face her father over the revelation about her love, she realized that it wouldn't be right to let Joshua face it all alone. Eventually she began to walk behind him. She hoped that by the time she arrived, the conversation between Joshua and her father would be over.

Chapter 3

Joshua wasn't really sure how to handle the upcoming conversation he was about to have with Karen's father. Karen and Joshua had been friends since they were little. Being neighbors and living in the kind of community they did, it's something that just happened. It was only a matter of time before the friendship blossomed into something more. For Karen and Joshua, it was a few months ago that things had changed between them. It was a natural evolution, one they both welcomed.

The goal was to see where things went between them for a little bit, and take it slow. What they found is that they truly felt something for each other. But before Joshua could go to Karen's father and tell him what was going on, her father had decided to marry Karen off.

Joshua couldn't exactly blame him. He didn't know what was really going on with Karen, how could he? They'd purposely left everyone in the dark so as to not cause a fuss. Now that the plan had backfired, it was Joshua's job to fix it.

He saw the farm approaching and took in a deep breath. There was a pang of anxiety in his stomach, but he said a silent prayer to the Lord in his mind and continued on. If it was meant to be, God would help Joshua succeed.

He opened the gate to the farm, braced himself, and went inside.

"Ah Joshua, come in. How may I help?" Karen's father Samuel closed the Bible that he was reading and welcomed the new guest.

Joshua took a deep breath. "Er. It's about your daughter."

"Karen," Samuel narrowed his eyes as he remembered the argument of the previous night. "Well, what about her?"

Joshua decided to dive right in before courage deserted him. "Karen and I like each other. We want your blessings for our marriage."

Joshua could see that Samuel was stunned. He tried to say something but couldn't speak. Joshua continued, "I know this may seem sudden, but I thought its best that you know about it. Karen and I have talked about it, and I am sure we would be happy in matrimony."

"I am sorry. That is not possible." Samuel finally found his voice. "I have already promised Karen's marriage to someone else."

"But, Karen likes me."

"Be that as it may, but the decision has been taken."

Joshua felt like he was sinking in quicksand. "But, the wedding hasn't happened yet. You can still call it off."

Samuel's nostrils flared. "Young man, this is a commitment I have made, and I will abide by it. My word is my honor, and I will uphold my honor."

***

Joshua lumbered back step by step through the field. Half way through his journey he met up with Karen. She must have been taking her time, because she should have been back at the house by the time he'd finished talking to her father.

She looked up at him with hopeful eyes. "How did it go?"

Joshua stayed silent for a moment. Then he shook his head. "Your father understood. But he'd already made a promise and he wasn't going to break it. It would go against what he believed in."

Karen was crushed. "Are you sure?"

Joshua nodded. "I did everything I could. I'm sorry."

Karen hung her head. "Thank you." She finally said. Then she continued to her farm to do the daily chores.

Joshua felt terrible. He'd done everything he could, but he still felt like he'd failed. He couldn't think of life without Karen. In the space of a few months, she had become his everything. And now he was about to lose her to another.

On his way back to his farm he prayed. He asked God to give him some kind of solution to bring their love together.

Please God, show us the light in this endless tunnel.

Chapter 4

Samuel wasn't sure whether he was angry or sad.

He was angry that Karen and Joshua hadn't told him about themselves. He was surprised to find that they had even discussed marriage. *And not once did they bother to inform him.* Joshua was a nice kid, and he had seen the disappointment on his face when he had declined his proposal. And that made him sad. Karen too would be unhappy with his decision, he thought. But she was an Amish lady, and she would learn to handle life's ups and downs with grace.

There was a knock on the door.

Samuel wondered if Joshua had come back, trying a last ditch attempt to make him change his mind. He opened the door. It was Mark.

"Mark! Welcome." Samuel was surprised to see Mark at his house. He tried to push Joshua out of his mind. "What brings you here?"

Mark smiled shyly. "Well, I feel we need to have a talk about Karen."

Samuel's brow furrowed. "What do you mean?"

"Well, in the shortest of terms, I no longer want to marry your daughter." The words felt odd coming out of Mark. And it hit Samuel like a ton of bricks.

Samuel's face went red. "What do you mean?"

Mark repeated his statement, but it didn't seem to be helping. Samuel still appeared to be simmering.

"I don't understand." He said to Mark. "All of a sudden? Why would you do this?"

Mark shook his head. "I can't really say. But I feel that God has spoken to me and that it's not right for me to marry Karen."

Samuel was furious. "I demand an answer. You can't just walk into my home and tell me you no longer want to marry my daughter."

"You can't help how you feel about someone. The simple answer is I don't like

Karen." Mark said.

"You arrogant fool." Samuel bristled with rage. "Get out of my house. I don't want to see you around here again."

Mark bowed his head. "Of course." He turned around and left the house.

***

Mark saw Karen working in the field. He thought that she deserved to know. He walked over and smiled at her. "Hello, Karen."

Karen gave him a polite, but reserved smile. "Hello, Mark."

"I need to discuss something." Mark said.

Karen avoided eye contact with him and nodded. "Okay."

"I talked with your father. I've called the marriage off." He said.

Karen blinked. "I'm sorry?" She said. She couldn't believe what she was hearing.

Mark gave a faint smile. "I overheard Joshua's conversation with your father. I like you, Karen. I had come here to help you with the harvest, and in the process get to know you better. I had felt that you were trying to avoid me. It was only today that I finally understood the reason. It's clear your heart is with another man, and it wouldn't be right for me to get in the way of that." Mark spread his arms in a grand gesture. "And therefore, I decided to set you free."

The more he spoke, the more Karen's face

brightened. "You should go talk to your father. Tell him to reconsider what you want. I'm sure he'll listen to you now."

Karen threw herself at Mark, wrapping her arms around him. "Thank you. This means so much to me."

Mark returned the embrace, still smiling. "Of course. You deserve to be happy. Now, go to your father, before he decides on another man."

Chapter 5

Karen returned to her house. She found her father sitting in the main room. His head was resting on his hands.

The floorboards creaked as she stepped, alerting him to her presence. He turned to her and sighed. "Sit down, Karen."

She took a seat across from him. She wasn't sure if she should say anything or wait for him. There was a moment of awkward silence between them. The argument from last night was fresh in both of their minds.

"I am sorry about yesterday." Samuel finally said.

"I apologize too, Father. I said some

things that I shouldn't have."

"There is something you should know. Mark called off the marriage. Did you say something to him?"

Karen realized that Mark must not have told him anything about Joshua. She shook her head. "No, I just met him after he left the house."

Samuel nodded. "All right."

Karen spoke up. "Would you consider Joshua then?"

Samuel sighed. "You know, I've known Joshua since you guys were kids. I would have considered him if I hadn't already promised you to Mark."

"You should have asked me who I wanted. We could have avoided this whole thing entirely." Karen said.

Samuel nodded. "You're right. I'm sorry. You're my daughter and I should have taken your advice on the matter. But that's all in the past now. I give you my blessing to marry Joshua."

Karen smiled from ear to ear. She hugged her father. "Thank you, Father. I can't tell you how much this means to me." Tears of joy streamed down her face.

Samuel rested his cheek on her head. God worked in mysterious ways. Samuel had been angry at Mark, but now, on seeing her daughter's happiness, he realized that the Lord had shown him the right path in the end.

***

Karen ran out of the house. She ran as fast she could over the field towards Joshua's farm. Joshua saw her coming from afar. He could see a wide smile on her face. Joshua wondered what had happened to her.

Karen came to her side all out of breath. "You... me..." She gesticulated with her hands.

Joshua couldn't understand. "What happened?"

Karen took a deep breath and then spoke, "Mark... heard you speak with Father. He called off the wedding. Father then agreed to our wedding."

"What!" Joshua couldn't believe it.

"Yes. It's true. We are going to get

married."

Joshua grasped Karen and hugged her tightly. After everything that had happened, Karen was back in his life again. He looked up at the sky and could see God's benevolence everywhere.

Thank you my Lord for straightening our paths.

***

AMISH BLIND LOVE

Chapter One

Rachel couldn't see anything, not even her own hand in front of her face. In fact, she was trapped inside her own world; all she had was darkness. While others happily enjoyed *rumspringa*, Rachel sat at home amongst her younger siblings, wishing she could see what they could see, hoping that one day she would be able to see more than her limitations.

Surprisingly, she was able to do many of the things that people considered useful like cooking, cleaning and even some sewing but still Rachel did not feel secure. Her parents tended to treat her with extra special care and as a result, she thought she would never be normal. And her neighbors, the ones she grew up with, didn't help at all. In fact, they added to her insecurity by saying things like, "Are you sure you're up to it with your condition?" Or "Do you think somebody like you will ever get married?"

And that was probably what bothered her most, the possibility of never getting married; because she wanted a family, a big one and up to this point it seemed very unlikely. Her *mudder* told her to ignore such comments and to trust God's judgment.

"Maybe *Gott* doesn't want you to marry, Rachel. Maybe you will find other ways to contribute to the community. Maybe He will use you for his service," her *mudder*, Elizabeth said.

But Rachel's heart was broken and she

didn't want to find other ways. She wanted to know now and she needed to know if she would ever be and ever feel normal.

"Yes," was her mother's reply but Rachel knew better. Deep inside, she wished that her life and her circumstances would both change at the same time.

"*Gott*, make me over again," she prayed as she touched her eyes.

Her parents often felt sorry for her because although she was their firstborn but the way it looked, she would be the last one married, if ever. Three of her younger siblings had married and gone on to start lives of their own and Rachel was left with the last two children of the family.

Sometimes her parents led her out to the porch to sit in the sun. She loved the feel of the sun's warmth on her face and she liked the feel of her bare feet in the grass.

She had been born blind and even after her parent tried to explain it to her, she never understood why. But it wasn't until she was older that she started to really feel that she was different. After enduring all the whispers and ridicule of her classmates and neighbors, Rachel began to get stronger. She learned to let the insults and the patronizing attitudes roll off of her and she learned how to spend most of her time alone.

"Why don't you go next door and see the neighbor's girls?" Elizabeth would say.

But Rachel would just shrug her shoulders. She had absolutely no interest in the neighbors' girls because they had hurt her so many times before. Even with her siblings, she had no one she could really depend on. There was one exception, of course, her Aunt May, who she was very close to.

Aunt May was a young widow woman who always found time to spend with her, even when others pushed her aside.

When Rachel entered May's kitchen, she heard May's voice, "Rachel, are you here?"

"Yes, Aunt May. I'm here,"

"It's a beautiful day so why are you sitting inside? Come out and at least feel the rain on your skin," May said.

"But the rain will make me wet."

"It's wet but the rain brings life. It makes the plants grow. It helps us to have water to drink and bathe and cook; the rain sustains life. The rain is a gift from *Gott*."

"Thank you," Rachel replied. "I never thought about it quite like that."

"Don't ever feel sorry for yourself, Rachel. It never helps. You are a beautiful young girl. It's only that you cannot see how wonderful you look."

Rachel smiled and felt better about herself.

May continued, "You must push yourself to reach your potential."

"Yes, Aunt May. I will do that."

One day, Rachel decided to go out for a walk in the rain. She started by going through the bushes in her yard, then venturing out, stepping into puddles which she found to be fun and splashing through the wet trees. She had to be careful not to lose her way; otherwise she wouldn't be able to find a way back home. So she took mental notes on the smell and feel of specific trees and rocks along her route. When it began to thunder, Rachel decided to leave, but as she turned she ran into a foreign object on the ground and lost her balance.

"Oh," she yelled as she tried to grab hold of something. But there was nothing in arm's reach and Rachel found herself sliding helplessly down the side of the hill.

Chapter Two

Jonah still remembered the flames lapping around him, eating up every piece of furniture in his bedroom and beginning to claim the walls also. The smoke was thick and he was choking. He called out to his parents, screaming as loud as he could but he wasn't sure that they could hear him. Finally, just as the flames had begun to close in on him, he could feel a hand pulling him out of his room and throwing him into the night air. Thankfully, he'd landed safely in a pile of hay intended to be brought into the barn the next morning. Still he'd suffered third-degree burns to his legs and feet and managed to break his legs during the fall; that was fourteen years ago.

Now at twenty-two Jonah looked in the mirror and all he saw was pain. The scars had faded out, but for him it was still real and he could still feel them; after all there was no going back to change the outcome of the worst night of his life. He looked at himself sideways, scrutinizing his face, checking the barely visible scars. But the scars on his legs and feet served as a reminder and although the wounds had left him with a slight limp, it was the least of his problems. Most of all, though, there was the scar on his heart, the one that missed his father and often wished his father hadn't risked his own life to save his.

"Jonah, where are you?"

"I'm coming, *mudder*," Jonah answered.

Jonah was an only child since his father was consumed by the fire on that fateful night and his *mudder*, who had problems with fertility, never remarried. He'd missed having siblings when he was growing up, but of course he'd adjusted to it and became a very sensitive boy. After moving away from the community with his *mudder* after the fire, and spending much of his life in the Midwest, his *mudder* finally decided to return to her home community.

New to the community, Jonah had many challenges. Yet, his biggest one was that he was still not married. He had gotten baptized a few months back but hadn't been lucky enough to find a bride for the wedding season.

Jonah had gone on a buggy ride with one girl, but it hadn't ended well. The girl didn't seem interested in him, and he believed she had rejected him because of his scars and limp. After that, he had all but given up on romance. He decided that he would just spend time in *Gott's* service before he settled down. Perhaps, then he'd be able to find the right girl or at least resign himself to being a hermit, which was what his mother lovingly called him. *Jonah, the hermit.*

"Jonah, don't you want to spend some time with your friends at the singing on Sunday?"

"*Mudder*, I have too much work to do

around the farm."

"But how will you ever meet someone if you're always at home?"

"I will, *mudder*, at the right time," he insisted.

"You know it's not healthy to spend so much time alone," she said, lines of worry forming across her forehead.

"But I am not alone. *Gott* is with me." And Jonah smiled at his *mudder* and went his way.

"You know, Jonah, one of these days you have got to forget what the fire did to you. I know you think that the fire has scarred your face, but it's not true. The scars have gone and you no longer look like the kid that we pulled out of the fire. Your father would want you to marry and have a good life," his *mudder* called after him.

Jonah listened but he didn't believe that he would ever be able to get past the fire.

Chapter Three

It was a cool autumn morning when Jonah left his house for an early morning walk. Walking always cleared his mind and he was able to pray as well. He liked to do this before his mother got up and before he started the farm chores. Although the farm they owned was small,there was no lack of work to be done.

Jonah walked down the road and through a clearing in the woods. He wondered where it led to. He took each step carefully because today's journey was over some rugged terrain. Before he knew it, the thunder cracked in the sky and the sound of it startled him. Starting to walk more briskly, or at least as fast as he could, but as he came upon a ditch, he heard a moan. There beneath a pile of rubble he noticed a girl. Immediately he jumped down and began to pull her out.

"Are you okay?" he asked.

"No," she said, breathing hard.

He carried her up to safety and seeing that she was covered with cuts and bruises, placed her on the grass, attempting to tend to her wounds. He ripped off his jacket, tore it into pieces and began to use it to make bandages for her arm and legs.

"My name is Jonah and I'm new here. Well actually, I'm not totally new but I have been away for a while and now I'm back."

"Oh, I see," Rachel said, listening

carefully.

Jonah peered at her. "And who are you?"

"I'm Rachel and I don't live far from here," she said, nodding. "I've heard about a new family coming."

"Well, it's actually just my mother and I. We've come back to stay with my *grohsmudder* after being gone for many years."

Rachel reached up and touched his face and neck, which made him feel awkward. He couldn't figure out why she was doing it but he tried to ignore it. Her hands were soft and felt good against his skin. She also smelled like lavender which distracted him for a few minutes.

Eventually he asked, "Are you ready to

follow me now?"

"Not really," she said.

"Why not? Are you unable to walk?"

"No, but I am blind,"she said.

And for a moment there was nothing but silence between them.

"Oh, I'm so sorry," Jonah said.

"Don't be sorry. It's not your fault." Rachel smiled.

Jonah was happy that she was smiling but he really didn't know what to say. He had never met anyone that was blind before.

"I mean don't be so sad about it... after all, you didn't have anything to do with it, did you?" Rachel chuckled.

But Jonah did not laugh. "Well, I... no

but…"

"If you will guide me, I will be happy to follow you." Rachel held onto his arm.

As Jonah began to understand, he nodded. "So that's how you fell in the first place?"

"You could say that. I just wanted a little adventure; but not like this."

They both began to laugh and as they walked, they continued to talk; he quickly realized that she was smart and easy to talk to. Jonah couldn't remember the last time he had enjoyed somebody's company as much as he did hers. And on top of that, she had the prettiest smile he'd seen in a long time.

But once they reached her front door, a

tall, burly man with a thick beard met them outside on the porch. He had quite an unwelcoming look on his face. "What are you doing with my daughter?"

"*Daed*, he saved me," Rachel tried to explain.

Jonah took a deep breath before answering. "I apologize for coming to your door like this but I found your daughter and she had fallen…"

Abraham cut him off. "*Denki* and you be on your way now."

Before Jonah could introduce himself or say another word, he found that her *daed* had pulled his daughter inside, and had closed the door in his face.

Chapter Four

Rachel's heart began to race. She had never seen her *daed* so angry before and she didn't know exactly how to react.

"What in the world were you doing with that boy in the woods?" Abraham paced the floor.

Rachel shook her head and waved her hands. "Nothing, *Daed*. I promise."

"Why did you go out there all alone?" Abraham rubbed his beard, anxiously.

"I wanted to do something different to have some adventure; for once just to have a little fun." Rachel spoke softly.

"We are not here for fun but for service to

Gott," her mother, Elizabeth reprimanded. "Don't you know that by now?"

Rachel could hardly respond quickly enough but her mother and father continued to scold her.

"What were you thinking? You could've been killed," Abraham said.

"And to come back in the arms of a stranger – just shameful." Elizabeth folded her arms against her chest.

"But he was nice enough to rescue me when I fell and I am grateful to him," Rachel explained.

"But we don't even know him," Abraham huffed.

"He must be new around here," Elizabeth

added.

"*Jah*, he is new but what difference does it make if he saved my life?" Rachel was disappointed in her parent's lack of understanding.

"*Gott* spared your life – not the stranger," Elizabeth spat out.

"And why were you out there on your own anyway?" Abraham asked.

Rachel paused for a moment. "Well, May told me that…"

"I should've known that your sister would have something to do with it," Abraham said, looking at his wife.

Rachel spoke quietly, "I wanted to do more with my life; I wanted to do what the normal people do."

"But you are normal, Rachel," Elizabeth said.

"But no one treats me that way. For once, I would like to be just the girl, not the blind girl." Rachel dropped her head.

"Well, that can never happen because you will always be blind. You were born that way; so you and your aunt had might as well accept it." Abraham turned his back on her and walked away.

Tears began to run down Rachel's face. Then her parents, without another word, left the room, slamming the door behind them. And Rachel dropped down in despair. *Gott, please help me, change me. Make me brand new.*

The rest of the day Rachel thought about the kind stranger and how friendly he had been. She remembered the conversation and the way he was able to put her at ease. She touched her eyes and imagined what he must've looked like.

She even made up her mind that she would find a way to meet him again. But after a moment, she realized that she didn't even know where he lived and even if she did how could she get there without anyone knowing? In fact, the more she thought about it, the more impossible it sounded, and in her grief she called out, "I want a normal life."

The next day Rachel and her family rose early for the neighborhood barn raising.

"Let's go, Rachel. We'll have to be there

early." Elizabeth gathered the food and carried it out to the buggy.

"Yes, *mudder*," Rachel said, straightening her dress and bonnet.

Within minutes they were pulling up in front of a house by the creek. Almost all of the neighbors were there also, getting prepared to work. Rachel helped her mother and the other women set up the tables with the food. She was also happy to meet her aunt May and to be able to spend all day with her.

Her two younger siblings circled her and one playfully said, "Which one am I?"

"And how do you know who I am?" the other one said.

"Don't tease your sister," Elizabeth said.

But Rachel was used to being mocked and it had become a part of her life.

May said, "Go on now. That's not a nice thing to do to your sister, knowing that she can't see." May shook her head and frowned.

"It's all right. It doesn't bother me anymore," Rachel said.

"I don't believe that." May patted Rachel lightly on the back.

That was what she loved about May; she understood her when no one else did. Rachel smiled inwardly.

"Don't you let these children make you feel bad," May said, before moving away to help the other women.

Finally, the men had finished unloading

the building materials and started to line up for their work assignments. To her surprise, Rachel heard Jonah's voice behind her. She couldn't see him but she would recognize that voice anywhere. She couldn't believe that he was actually here at the barn raising too. Her heart leaped with anticipation as she could hardly wait to get his attention. She could tell which direction the voice was coming from, but of course, she couldn't tell exactly where or what he was doing or how far away he was. There was nothing she could do but wait and wait she did.

Chapter Five

Once it was time for lunch to be served Rachel waited patiently as the lines formed. Plate after plate she helped to prepare, waiting to hear the familiar sound she longed for. And it seemed like forever, waiting for what might not happen.

Finally, feeling exhausted, she sat down next to a tree. It was then that she heard footsteps approaching her. She heard an audible breathing but she didn't dare say a word.

"I can't believe that you are here. It is a miracle," Jonah said.

Rachel could hear the smile in his voice and she was pleased. "I'm happy to see you again too."

Rachel could also sense the quiet around her but she couldn't take the chance that no one was watching until she was sure.

Jonah suggested, "Would you take a little walk with me while no one is watching?"

It was just what she wanted to hear and she slipped her hand into his as he led her away from the crowd.

Rachel giggled, and then covered her mouth. "How did you manage to get me away?"

It wasn't easy but ever since I saw you standing over here, I'd planned to come over at the right time, the quietest time," he said. "Everyone is full and tired now. Most people are closing their eyes for a bit of rest."

Rachel chuckled. "It was very smart of you to come now."

"I can't take credit for that," Jonah said. "I had to see you again and I get the feeling that your parents don't approve."

Rachel made a sad face. "That's an understatement."

Jonah shrugged. "But what have I done?"

"It's not you. It's just that since I was born blind, they've been very overly protective of me and..."

"I can certainly understand that. I guess if I had a daughter as beautiful as you, I'd want to protect her too," he said.

But I am not a doll for protecting," she countered.

"Oh, no, I didn't mean it like that. I can see that you are very strong and I can't understand why your parents can't see that too."

Rachel kicked the dirt on the ground. "I don't know why *they* can't see when *I* am the one who is blind."

"Maybe they are afraid and they don't want to see," Jonah said.

"Maybe you're right about that. What about you? What has brought you back to Lancaster?"

"When I was small, my *daed* passed away in a house fire. We left because of the memories. It really took a big toll on us. My mother couldn't stand it here but now it's different for her," Jonah explained.

Rachel took his hand and squeezed it. "But you didn't say that it was different for you. Does being here still bother you?"

"I must be honest. Yes, it still keeps me up at night," he said. "But believe it or not since I've met you, you have helped to make me feel more comfortable here than I've been." Jonah peeked through the trees.

"What is it? I can feel you looking away?" Rachel sensed that Jonah was no longer talking in her direction.

"The men are beginning to go back to work," Jonah said.

"Then we must go back," she said, panicking.

"Don't worry; I will lead you back," Jonah

said, grabbing her hand and guiding her back safely, while he carefully walked in the other direction.

Jonah turned around just in time to see Rachel's *mudder* tap her on the shoulder.

"Rachel?..."

Chapter Six

Rachel gasped as her *mudder* stood in front of her with her arms crossed. She swallowed hard.

"Where have you been? I've been looking all over for you. Let's get this food wrapped and put away," Elizabeth said

Rachel sighed with relief. "Sorry, *mudder*, but I stepped away for a moment."

"Well, let's get busy, shall we? No time to waste here. The men will be hungry again soon," Elizabeth said, handing Rachel a pot.

Rachel was so happy that she had not been caught that she clasped her hands together and looked up to the heavens. *Thank you.*

Yet, just as she was wrapping the food May came over to her and whispered in her ear," The next time you decide to disappear into the woods with a stranger, you'd better be more careful."

"You know?"

"I don't know anything except that I saw you two leave together," May said, turning her head sideways, which was one of her favorite things to do when she was confused.

"He saved my life yesterday," Rachel said.

May asked, "Oh, is he the young man who brought you home after the fall?"

"*Jah*, I see that *mudder* has passed the word on," Rachel said. She couldn't see her aunt's expressions but she was almost certain that she was staring at Jonah.

"He looks to be a nice person. I am happy for you but make sure that if you two are going to be courting that you make it official," May said.

"I don't know if that's possible," Rachel said.

May's voice was soft and understanding. "It is still *rumspringa* for you and how else will you ever marry if you don't get out of the house and meet people?"

Rachel shrugged her shoulders but secretly took into consideration what her aunt had said.

The very next day was Sunday, but not

just any Sunday, it was church Sunday. Rachel found her best dress at the back of her closet and twirled around in it before going downstairs to help her *mudder* with breakfast.

"You're looking mighty pretty this morning," Elizabeth complimented. "What's the occasion?"

"No occasion. I just wanted to wear my favorite dress," she said. "Well, actually I was thinking about the singing this evening."

Elizabeth squinted her eyes at her daughter as she cracked the eggs into the pan. "You want to go?"

Rachel spun around, then feeling a little dizzy, grabbed the table to brace herself. "I think I should. I want to be normal, after all."

"But I don't know if that's such a good idea to get your hopes up like that…"

"I am a big girl; *mudder* and you can't protect me forever. If I get my feelings hurt, then I will survive," Rachel said.

"I suppose," Elizabeth agreed, reluctantly.

During the first half of the church service, Rachel had no way of knowing whether or not Jonah was there, but once lunch was served, Jonah found a way to quickly pass by Rachel and whisper in her ear. It made her whole body shiver and she kept her secret close to her heart until church was completely over.

Rachel could hardly wait for the opportunity to be with Jonah, but her parents were still around. She waited patiently for them to finish their friendly conversations and leave in the family buggy. Then she went back down to the basement and sat on the bench with the other young people. She hoped that Jonah understood that she would be staying for the singing and she hoped that he wanted to stay too.

Within minutes, her worries were over as Jonah sat down with the group and began to sing. Rachel, too, joined in, and in between they talked and laughed with each other.

"This has been the most fun I've had in a long time," he said.

Rachel confronted him with, "Have you allowed yourself to have fun before this?"

Jonah shook his head. "No, I haven't."

Rachel asked, "So what has been holding

you back?"

"I don't know but I know that you've helped to give me hope again," Jonah said.

"Oh, come on. You just met me."

"But you're so bright and full of life. You don't have sight but yet you have so much insight." Jonah hit his fit against his hand to illustrate his point. "You don't let anything break you down."

"I did for a long time but my Aunt May, helped me to get better." Rachel put her hands over her eyes. "She taught me that even though I'm blind, I can still do many things for myself and I can." Rachel took her hands down. "But now I want…"

"What is it that you want?" Jonah asked.

"I want to have a normal life like everyone else. I do not want to be pampered or put to the side. I want to live my life to the fullest." Rachel smiled her biggest smile.

"That sounds like a good way to be," Jonah said.

"If only I can get my parents to see it that way too," Rachel said, looking around her.

Chapter Seven

Jonah could hardly believe the way he was enjoying Rachel's company. Her smile and joy seemed to bring him out of his depression. Whenever he was with her, he could forget about his past and think about the future. He didn't know exactly what it was about her that he appreciated more, but he was clearly captivated by her inner beauty and strength. And because she couldn't see him, he for once felt comfortable in a woman's presence without worrying about how the other person perceived his appearance. Sadly, it was time for the evening to end but he didn't want to let her go.

"May I bring you home in my buggy?" he

asked.

"That would be a very bold move," she said. "But *jah*, you may."

Jonah smiled and helped her into the buggy. And as he steered the horses, she sang to him.

"You have such a beautiful voice," he said. "But I hardly heard you over the others earlier."

Rachel cast her eyes downward. "I always quiet down in the presence of others. It's something I've always done."

"But why?"

"I guess I don't feel good enough so I hide," Rachel explained, using her hands to tell what was in her heart.

"You hide your voice?"

"I hide everything about me." Rachel wiped a solitary tear from her eye. "But I can be myself around you. I don't know why but I can."

"Starting now, there will be no more hiding. You will be yourself and that's all. *Gott* will protect you. He will protect us both."

"And what about you? What are you going to do about burying the past?"

"I'm still working on that but you're right though." Jonah nodded.

The two of them held hands until they reached Rachel's front door.

Jonah chuckled. "I don't dare walk you to the front door."

"Oh, come on, you must. No hiding,

remember?" Rachel pulled Jonah along with her.

Jonah's heart began to speed up as they knocked on the door. He could see the light from the kerosene lamps burning in the window.

"Don't be afraid," Rachel said.

But Jonah was shaking because he was not looking forward to a confrontation with her oversized *daed*.

As expected, Abraham answered the door but before he could get the chance to say something, Jonah went up to him and introduced himself.

"My name is Jonah Yoder. I brought your daughter here from the singing."

Abraham was stunned and didn't say a word. But his eyes moved from one to the other taking in the situation.

Rachel interjected, "Jonah brought me home tonight because we like each other and we'd like to court."

Elizabeth entered the room just as Rachel had started the last sentence and looked faint. By the time Rachel finished, Elizabeth fell back and Abraham caught her.

Jonah took two steps back just in case there was any trouble but added." I am very fond of your daughter. I think that she is beautiful and we would like to spend time together, with your permission, of course.

Abraham and Elizabeth looked at each other and then looked at Jonah.

Abraham walked right up to Jonah's face.

"Do you really think that I would let you be with

my daughter? The answer is no."

Chapter Eight

Jonah couldn't believe what he had just heard. Abraham looked as if he was fuming; he stood, leaning over Jonah, pointing his finger into Jonah's face. Jonah was shaking with fear. If only this hadn't happened. If only he could turn back the hands of time and start over again, he would never have agreed to come inside. What had he been thinking?

"I apologize for intruding but I only have the most honest intentions," Jonah said.

"How could you possibly have honest intentions with a blind girl? She has special needs and she will need special attention for the rest of her life." Abraham spat out.

"Then perhaps I am the one who will give that to her. I would like to get to know your daughter better and perhaps ask for her hand in marriage," Jonah explained.

Abraham shook his head and put up his hand. "My daughter is not ready to marry; that is a big responsibility."

Rachel offered, "But, *Daed*, what if I am ready?"

"How can you be ready when you cannot see the things around you?" Abraham asked.

Rachel walked up to her *daed*. "But you once told me that I will always be blind; that I cannot change. But I am ready to live a new life, and I know I can live. I can do anything I put my mind to, even without sight."

"I've learned, in this short time, that your daughter is very strong, stronger than you may think," Jonah said.

Elizabeth moved towards Jonah. "How do you know so much about it?"

Jonah looked at Elizabeth and then at Abraham. He took a deep breath, looked at Rachel and said, "I know because I am learning to love your daughter."

Chapter Nine

Not surprisingly, Abraham asked Jonah to leave and banned him from the house. At first Rachel was heartbroken, but when Jonah turned up at her home, throwing twigs at her window late one evening, she snuck out to meet him under a willow tree.

They spent that evening and the next few evenings together in the same spot, talking until it was nearly dawn. Finally, after quite a few weeks of the same routine, meeting here and there in the shadows, professing their love to one another, they decided that it was time to tell their parents that they wanted to get married.

Of course, Jonah's mother was happy that

her son had found someone to love. But they knew that Rachel's parents would not be that easy.

"We will find a way to be together, no matter what," Jonah said.

"I hope you're right," Rachel answered, reluctantly. She just wasn't sure about what her parent's reaction to their news would be. She admitted that it didn't look promising.

"We will pray and *Gott* will make a way for us to be married. I'm sure of it. You have taught me about courage and strength. You have taught me to be confident. I can finally forget my scars of yesterday and look forward to tomorrow."

"But how can I inspire you when I'm just

a little blind girl," she asked.

"You have never been just a little blind girl. You are a courageous and exceptional woman and I would be proud to be your husband," Jonah said.

"I hope that I can live up to your expectations," Rachel said.

"My only expectation is that you love me for the rest of our lives and I will take care of you. But most importantly, you can take care of yourself." Jonah swallowed hard. "You always could."

"Can we really do this?"

"Together I'm confident that we can." Jonah took her hand and just as they were about to walk up to the house, they heard a rustling in the bushes.

Chapter Ten

Rachel held her breath but was relieved to see that it was only her aunt May.

"What are you doing here?" Rachel asked.

"You came to me last night in a dream and asked me for help so I figured I'd better hurry up and see what the matter was," May explained.

"We are going in to announce our engagement. We've been secretly seeing each other ever since my father said that we couldn't and we are ready to stop hiding," Rachel said.

"We are in love," Jonah said, kissing Rachel on the cheek.

May nodded. "Then I suppose that's what I'm here for, to help your parents to understand and to let go."

Rachel and Jonah went up to the door, arm in arm and May followed closely behind. This time Elizabeth opened the door but when she saw the two of them, her face softened and she began to laugh. Rachel didn't know what to think of it.

But the three of them stood by the door waiting for Abraham to come out. Although Abraham's initial response was negative, they eventually wore him down. May did most of the talking on behalf of the couple, and reiterated that Rachel was no longer a child, but a grown up woman.

"I only want you to be happy," Abraham said.

"I am happy, *daed*," Rachel confirmed.

And the five of them discussed their wedding plans as Rachel and Jonah excitedly displayed their love. There was no more hiding and no more insecurity. There was only love and acceptance. Rachel would be married and have the normal life she'd always dreamed of and Jonah could finally get rid of the nightmare that haunted him for years. And although it had started off a little shaky, eventually the entire family and the community were able to celebrate their impending union.

Rachel and Jonah danced to the beat of their own drummer on their wedding day.

Everyone whispered about the stranger and the blind girl, but the couple didn't care what anyone thought about them anymore. Rachel looked up to the heavens on her wedding day. She couldn't see but she could feel the warmth of the sun on her face.

Gott, thank you for making me brand new.

***

AMISH SYMPHONY

Chapter 1

Isaac woke up in the middle of the night and stretched. He quietly stepped out of his bed and lit a candle. Then he pulled on his pants and raised his window. He climbed out onto the ledge, and although his footing was shaky, he was able to maneuver himself from his second-floor window down to the ground. He ran through the bushes and he didn't look back.

Once he reached the secret place in the field, he got down to the ground and started to dig, with the stick at first and then with his hands. Finally, he snatched it out of the dirt, dusted it off and checked the batteries to see if it was still working. He stuck the earbuds into his ears and pressed Play. A burst of loud music totally awakened him and he danced under the moonlight until he was tired. Finally, he rested on the grass listening to soft music until it was nearly dawn.

He dreamed that he was a famous rock star and that he had fans catering to his every whim. He slept peacefully as the words to songs appeared in his mind. They were crystal clear and in the dream, he had written them down. He sang about love and he sang about pain. But then someone came up to him and asked why he wasn't singing about *Gott*.

That was the way his dream ended, abruptly.

Isaac opened his eyes and realized that he

had fallen asleep outside. He hurried to bury the evidence, and climbed back up to his room before his parents found out what he had done.He would be in big trouble for sure.

It wasn't that during *Rumspringa*, Isaac's parents didn't expect a little rebellion, but being the respectful boy that he was, he tried to keep it to a minimum. No one was supposed to know that he owned an MP3 player.

He had purchased it on one of those nights when he had gone out to Walmart with his friend Samuel and had heard music playing over the loudspeaker for the first time. He remembered that he'd started dancing in the aisles, although he wasn't quite sure of what kind of dance he was doing. The music had so much life in it and the sound was so rich that Isaac was ecstatic. Before he knew it, he and Samuel were mouthing the words to the song and popping their fingers as they strolled down the aisles-two obviously Amish boys having the time of their lives. Later they realized that they must have looked peculiar to other people, but neither of them cared. It was the most magnificent feeling that Isaac could ever remember having. It was then that he knew that music was a part of him and that he could no longer be separated from it.

Isaac's parents always knew that he was a musical boy. Although singing was a regular ritual in most Amish households, for Isaac, it was always more. He would not only sing the traditional hymns or church songs but he'd also written the lyrics to songs of his own. He liked the freedom that creating his own music gave him. And since he didn't have any instruments, he tapped with his foot, his fingers, clapped his hands, pounded with sticks or rocks or anything he could think of to make music. He had a wonderful sense of melody and tune, and his parents finally bought him a harmonica to appease him. They let him play it on occasion, usually for special church services. It was finally deemed acceptable in his community but not in every Amish circle; the matter of whether or not to allow harmonicas had actually been widely debated throughout the country. So he played whenever he could and looked forward to singing in the men's choir at church. But unfortunately, in his community that was as far as his love for music could go.

Still his curiosity often got the best of him as he heard stories of singers and musicians who traveled the country and the world, singing and playing instruments of their choice, allowing music to infiltrate their lives. He found himself wishing for more freedom. Although he'd been Amish all his life, he couldn't understand what was so wrong about music and why they were so limited where learning about it, playing it, or listening to it was concerned. Sadly, no one understood his needs. Even his parents considered it a phase. "He'll grow out of it," they said, year after year. But Isaac never did; in fact his love of music only grew stronger and bigger on the inside of him.

Isaac changed into his work clothes and tidied up his bed. He didn't share a bedroom with anyone because his two brothers were older and had already gotten married and moved out of the house. He only had two sisters left in the house to contend with.

"Isaac, come downstairs now," Isaac's mother called.

Isaac hurried to get ready and ran down the stairs, "Good morning, *Mudder*."

"Isaac, hurry because your father and brothers have already left the house and breakfast will be ready for you soon." Isaac's mother and two sisters continued to prepare the morning meal and did not lose their rhythm.

Isaac ran outside to join his father and older siblings who every morning, came to work on their father's farm. Since it was such a large farm, they'd never had to purchase ones of their own; instead it had become the family business. As a cool breeze blew across Isaac's face, he looked up at the dark clouds forming in the sky. It looked like it was going to rain. As he toiled in the dirt, he thought of his music and hummed a little tune. He tapped his foot to the beat in his head which was a frequent past time of his.

"What are you doing?" His father, Jacob, asked.

"I'm just listening to tunes in my head." Isaac smiled.

His father frowned. "Keep your mind on your work."

"Yes, *Daed*," he agreed.

Isaac eyed his father curiously. "Why aren't we allowed to play instruments and enjoy music?"

Isaac remembered how he had asked his father for a violin when he was younger but he had been turned down. It was understood that instruments were not allowed but something in Isaac's spirit never rested well with that decision. On the inside, he'd been longing to play an instrument for years. When he was fourteen, his father rewarded him with a harmonica, and he was grateful but it was not the same as a violin, a piano or a bass guitar.

Although he'd only heard snatches of these sounds throughout the years, he knew enough to desire them.

"Where have you gotten these foolish ideas from? I know that it must be from running around with that foolish boy, Samuel." Jacob shook his head. "That boy is on his way to being excommunicated for not being baptized. His parents are heartbroken. Is that who you want to be associated with?"

Isaac was silent as he understood the rules of respect for his elders. However, he hated that his father had referred to his friend in a negative way. But there was nothing he could do about it. And he did respect the Amish values, despite Samuel's influence.

Jacob put his hand on his son's shoulder. "Isaac, get your mind off the things of the world; that's why we Amish have separated ourselves so we can stay focused. For right now, keep your mind on your work. You will find a nice girl and get married soon. I don't understand why you're not courting yet. *Rumspringa* is your time, your time."

"I've been going to the singings but I just haven't met the right girl yet," Isaac explained as he looked his father in the eyes.

True enough he had tried, once with a quiet girl who never talked and another time with a girl who loved to eat more than anything else. In both cases, after a few days of communication, he was disappointed with them because, besides being Amish, they didn't have much in common. He'd quickly broke it off with them, one at a time, and decided that he would rather have spent time with his family or alone. Better yet, he'd preferred to spend time with his music; if only he could listen to it out in the open. But that was impossible. Isaac's mind quickly returned to the present.

"Well, it's almost the middle of summer; there's not much time left for you to frolic around."Jacob pointed his finger at him."Get your head together so you can get baptized."

"What if I make another choice?" Isaac wasn't sure how to start this kind of conversation because he seldom had heart to heart conversations with his father. Mostly, they just worked together but they didn't talk.

Isaac's father rubbed his beard. "Being Amish is a good choice. It's a blessing from *Gott*."

"But it's not the only choice, *Daed*, is it? Doesn't *Gott* give us choices?"

His father raised his eyebrows, and then turned his back to Isaac as he continued to plow the land. He had ignored Isaac's question and Isaac felt hurt and alone on the inside. *Gott, why does no one understand me?*

And Isaac went back to listening to the music in his head, humming and tapping his foot. He sang to himself and he dreamed a variety of dreams. He kept these things hidden in his heart and he wondered if he and the things he loved would ever be free?

Chapter 2

Sarah walked across the campus with her books under her arm. After years of waiting for it, she was grateful to finally be able to complete her education. Now in her second year of college, she was ready to see her dream come to pass. And being a Christian music producer was the goal, at least for now.

She clicked her heels and walked into the cafeteria and ordered her lunch. As she left the cashier, she noticed her friend Marcy, sitting nearby and went over to sit by her.

"Hi, Sarah." Marcy smiled and slid over to make room for Sarah.

"Hi," Sarah said, setting her lunch tray on the table.

Marcy bit into an apple. "Are you done with classes for the day?"

Sarah made a funny face. "Yep, I sure am. Why?"

Marcy giggled. "Because I'm going to free concert on campus and I thought maybe we could go together."

"Oh I'm sorry. Actually, I have mid-week Bible study tonight."

"Oh, uh...that's nice," Marcy stuttered, awkwardly. "I thought you and your family gave up all that religious stuff when you left the Amish?"

Sarah shook her head. She didn't want to

offend Marcy but she felt compelled to explain. "It's not a religious thing; it's a personal relationship thing that I have with God. And one has nothing to do with the other."

Marcy nodded but Sarah could tell that she was still confused. She knew that her friend was not spiritual and struggled to find the words to help her comprehend.

Sarah continued, "You see, my parents left the Amish community because they wanted to become missionaries."

"Wow, that's very generous of them," Marcy said.

Sarah could see Marcy contemplating what she had said and so she continued, "Yes, they're in South America right now, feeding starving children and families."

"That's very commendable."

"Well…"

"I wish I had the courage to do something like that. It's such a worthy cause. I mean we have so much and some people have so little," Marcy said.

"That's very true and it's our mission to serve and help others," Sarah said, trying to be as clear as possible.

"A missionary trip sounds very cool. " Marcy nodded, and then she turned to her and asked, "Why don't you go with them?"

"Well, because I'm in school and besides I have a different calling – music."

"Cool. At least, you're sure about what

you want to do with your career. I know you've always been into music and stuff but me, I don't know…"

Sarah chuckled. "Yeah, I'm just unsure about everything else."

"What do you mean?"

Sarah shrugged her shoulders as she bit into her hamburger. "I'm still torn between the life in the world and the life I grew up with."

"Being Amish seems so plain, though. I mean, at least from the things I've seen and heard."

"First of all, don't believe everything you hear. And yes, a lot of it was plain but believe it or not there is a peace in it," Sarah said. "Now I'm struggling to fit into my new church and this new existence without rules and without structure."

"We have rules," Marcy interjected.

"Not as much as I'm used to. It's just not the same and I don't mean laws, but moral codes and a set of standards or values. Like we have the *ordnung* but the Amish have an order for everything. For example, I get up in the morning and I have one million choices of what to wear or how to wear my hair and what to do with my day."

"I see what you mean but choices are a good thing though, right?"

"Sometimes it is and sometimes it's not. I'm just trying to make sense of my life and find my way, without leaving *Gott*, I mean God, out the picture," Sarah explained.

Marcy squinted her eyes. "I'm not sure I understand what you mean."

Sarah smiled. "Don't worry about it. You'll never understand unless you've been Amish."

"You're a smart girl. I'm sure you'll find your way."

Sarah put ketchup on one of her french fries and stuck it into her mouth. "I hope so because I just received a letter from my parents who will be coming back soon."

"What's the problem with that?"

Sarah leaned in as if she was sharing a secret. "The problem is that they want me to join them on the next mission trip."

"Are you going to go with them?"

"I guess that would depend on what God's will is." Sarah sighed. "I'll have to pray and see if it will be music or missions for me."

Chapter 3

Isaac and his friend Samuel ran to the field and hopped into the buggy. Samuel steered the horse down the winding road, through the darkness and into town. Isaac was supposed to be at the singing but he had managed to sneak away right after his parents left the church service.

Sitting with the other young people his age singing and socializing, never yielded the results his parents and the Amish community had hoped for him. Everyone wanted him to meet a nice girl and get engaged but no one had really excited him. He figured that he was just different and because of that he dreamed differently. He didn't see things the way most others did. He'd never fit in with this peers once he got older. So he'd retreated to his own little private world where no one could enter.

Although he had attended school with Samuel as they were growing up, they had only really connected once Samuel refused to be baptized. Isaac wasn't sure why he was drawn to Samuel after that, but after a couple of secret rides into town, they were the best of friends.

Isaac chuckled with delight in seeing his only real friend. "Have you still been running around town?"

Samuel smacked his gum. "Every chance I get, I'm hoping to get out of here one day.

Don't you want out?"

"Not really," Isaac answered.

"Why not?"

Isaac considered it for a moment and realized it would be a lonely existence if he ever left. "It's not so bad. My whole family, aunts and uncles, and cousins are here. I wouldn't think of leaving."

"But what about all the things you say you want to do like your music and freedom?" Samuel stopped the wagon and they both got out. "Don't those things count?"

Samuel led the way into a little café, found a corner booth and sat down.

Isaac thought about the teachings of the church. Individual preferences never mattered.

"They count but *Gott's* will counts more."

Samuel shrugged. "Not so sure about the *Gott* thing either."

"My relationship with *Gott*; that's the one thing I am sure about," Isaac admitted.

Samuel nodded. "I'm glad you're so confident. I have lots of doubts."

"That's all I am confident about, though. Everything else is up in the air, blown away like dust." Isaac blew into his palm to illustrate his point.

Suddenly, Isaac spotted a waitress who had beautiful long, flowing blonde hair and hazel colored eyes. She was heading in their direction.

"Do you see how gorgeous she is? Isaac whispered.

"So, that's how these girls are out here on the outside," Samuel explained, pointing at other women in the establishment.

"No, I've seen others but none are as beautiful as her," Isaac said.

Samuel glanced over at the waitress who was coming towards them. "She's okay, I guess," Samuel whispered.

"You guess? She's perfect," Isaac said.

Samuel shrugged. "If you say so. Why don't you talk to her?"

The two of them spent a moment, bickering back and forth about whether or not Isaac should talk to the waitress. The next thing they knew, the waitress had approached their table.

She was wearing a blue and red waitress uniform. "How may I help the two of you this evening?" she asked.

"Ma'am, my friend here would like to talk to you …"

Isaac looked horrified and poked Samuel in the ribs with his elbow. "I uh…"

The waitress chuckled. "How are you? I see you're Amish, hmmm?"

Suddenly, Isaac was embarrassed as he remembered that his clothing spoke volumes about him.

"Yes, I am. I'm Isaac."

"Hello, Isaac. I'm Sarah and I noticed the

outfit," she said, smiling.

Isaac looked into her eyes, dreamily. "You recognized it right away, did you?"

"It's pretty hard to hide." She giggled. "Besides, I used to be Amish, a long time ago.

Now Isaac's curiosity was really peaked. "What do you mean by 'used to be'?"

"Well, my parents and I left the community about two and a half years ago. They're missionaries now."

Samuel yawned, and then excused himself to go play video games.

They both watched Samuel walk away and waited for the awkward silence to pass.

Isaac was very interested in what she had to say. He leaned forward in his seat."How did that work out for you? I mean how do you feel about it now?"

Sarah bent over a little and looked around to see if anyone was listening to their conversation before continuing, "At first I was really confused and I missed my extended family a lot, especially my *grosmudder* but I just did."

Isaac watched her expressions. "It must've been hard, though?"

Sarah nodded, but she kept a pleasant look on her face. "A little but the best thing has been me being able to go to college."

"Oh, what would you do there?"

"Why studying, of course, silly," She nudged him with her elbow. "I am studying music."

And those were just the magic words that Isaac needed to hear.

Chapter 4

As it turned out, Isaac spoke off and on for the rest of the evening. Samuel complained about feeling left out but neither of them paid him any attention. They were completely enamored with each other, speaking about music, the industry and Sarah's program of study. There was a lot to talk about, including their similar upbringings and traditional values. They also discussed the restrictions and contradictions they found in Amish society. Samuel yawned as if they were boring him the entire time.

When Sarah had her break, she was able

to sit down with them and share the story of how she'd been working her way through college, practically supporting herself, and that despite the hardships, she enjoyed it.

Sarah liked Isaac's smile; it seemed to light up the room.

"I promise that the next time I see you, I'll sing for you," Isaac said.

"That would be wonderful," she answered. "And maybe I'll dance for you."

"I've never met anyone like you before," Isaac said, smiling.

"Likewise," Sarah said. "It's been fun."

But soon it was time to go and Sarah feared she wouldn't see Isaac again. After all, she was on the outside.

They said their goodbyes and Sarah watched through the huge glass windows as Isaac and Samuel left in a buggy, heading down the winding road, back to the Amish community. She wondered what Isaac thought about their meeting and whether or not it was as rewarding for him as it was for her. She didn't know what it was about him but she was drawn to him in every way.

She'd left the Amish during *Rumspringa* and had never had the opportunity to find a mate. Once she was out in the world, there were new rules for male-female relationships and since she was used to much more structure, she didn't engage in much dating. She had a few male classmates that she would hang out with every now and then but she had never been involved in a committed relationship. Truthfully, she hadn't found anyone she was interested in being committed to.

All kind of things were going through her mind, like how she really wanted to help Isaac with his music career. In doing this, she'd suggested that he take a few classes but she knew that really wasn't possible until when and if he made a decision. If he didn't choose to leave like her family did, she knew there was a good possibility that she would never see him again.

Still Sarah continued to live her life, going to school and work, without a word of complaint. She wrote and played music in her spare time yet still found time to volunteer at the church. She'd brought her Amish values of service to community along with her. Every day she prayed that God's will be done in her life and she secretly hoped that Isaac would walk through that door again.

The following Sunday evening, he did just that and Sarah was thrilled. She ran up to him and hugged him. She could see by the look on his face that he was both excited and surprised by what she had done. She was pretty sure that he was not accustomed to that kind of open display of affection. Yet, he hugged her back and didn't seem to want to let go. But she managed to peel his hands off her as she reminded him that she was on duty and that her boss was watching.

"I'm sorry," he said. "I guess I just got carried away."

"I understand. It is good to see you too," Sarah said. "It's a little slow in here tonight so I'm going to ask if I can leave early. I have someone who can cover my tables and that way we can talk."

Isaac looked around them. "That would be great but are you sure you won't get into any trouble?"

"There is only one way to find out," Sarah said.

Sarah went behind the counter to speak to her boss and he agreed that she could leave early. She was so happy she could've screamed. She gathered her things and headed towards the front door, beckoning Isaac to follow.

Sarah looked around the parking lot. "So where is your buggy?"

"Nowhere," Isaac answered.

"Nowhere? How did you get here tonight?"

"Samuel dropped me off this time and left. He said I'd wasted his time last time we were out here," Isaac explained.

"I'll bet he did." Sarah threw her head back and laughed heartily.

"But I didn't care. I just had to see you again."

"That's really sweet." She pointed towards an old car. "Let's get in my car and I'll take you to our apartment. It's not that far from here."

While riding, Isaac explained to her how he slipped away from the group without being noticed, how he'd spent all week thinking about her and how she was the nicest girl he knew. Sarah was impressed with his politeness and intelligence.

Once they'd arrived at her parent's apartment, Isaac was reluctant to come in.

"Come on in. It's okay, really." Sarah pulled him by the hand. "There's no one here but me. I'll make us some coffee and we'll be able to talk in private."

"I do like the sound of that." So he came in, sat on the couch and began to relax.

Sarah sat beside him.

Isaac looked around the living room. "Everything is so different from what I'm used to. There are so many styles and patterns, and colors."

"Yes, that's one of the things I love about it-difference. Everything is not the same. I mean *Gott* made us all different didn't he?"

"I guess so. To be honest, I never really thought about it."

They sat and talked for hours over coffee.

"Would you like to listen to music?" she asked.

"I'd love to," Isaac said.

Sarah played several popular hits she thought he'd like, and then she sang for him and played her electric guitar. Before long, they were listening to slow songs on the radio and dancing cheek to cheek.

It was undoubtedly, the most romantic night of Sarah's life and she could tell that Isaac was enjoying himself too. But as they were holding each other close, Sarah began to feel bothered by it.

Sarah pulled herself apart from his arms. "Maybe we should stop holding each other so close?"

"Don't you like it?" Isaac asked.

"Very much so and that's the problem. I don't want to do anything that will be dishonorable. That's what I miss about having the Amish rules."

"You're right," he agreed. "The rules help

to keep us in order. Would you ever go back?"

Sarah backed away from him. "I think about it often and I sometimes feel that I might," she said.

"I'd like to see you again," Isaac said. "But I'm not sure that I can. They're putting pressure on me now to be baptized and to marry…"

"I understand. You'll have to do whatever you think is best," she said, solemnly.

"In fact, my father has told me that he is tired of waiting and that he will choose a mate for me if I do not."

"Will the Bishop allow it?"

"He might. I won't fight my parents."

Sarah nodded, with tears in her eyes.

Sarah dropped Isaac back at the restaurant where Samuel was waiting for him. She blew him a kiss and disappeared into the darkness.

If Isaac was forced to marry someone else, her heart would be broken but there was nothing she could do about it.

Chapter 5

That night Isaac found it difficult to sleep. He tossed and turned as he dreamed about Sarah. He also dreamed about the music that *Gott* had put in his heart. If he stayed, he would never be able to fulfill that dream but if he left, the vision could be complete. There was so much more he could learn about music on the outside and so much he could do in ministry.

He had discussed some of these things with Sarah and they had become closer because of it. She'd wanted to produce Christian music and he'd wanted to make Christian music. Both of them wrote songs and both of them wanted to serve *Gott* and their community. He could hardly believe what a blessing meeting her had been. She promised to sign him up for music classes and to take him around her school. And she was not only smart but beautiful. Meeting her had proven itself to be a dream come true. He knelt down and said a quiet prayer and when peace covered him, he closed his eyes and went to sleep.

He woke up to his mother's shaking. "Where have you been going the past two Sunday evenings?"

Isaac opened his eyes and saw both his mother and father standing over him. He knew that the façade was over.

"Someone has spotted you out and about

town at all ungodly hours of the night. "What are you doing?" Mary asked.

"I've been meeting a beautiful girl and I've been learning about music. I haven't been doing anything wrong." Isaac felt like a five year old instead of the soon to be twenty year old that he actually was.

"We'll be the judge of that," Jacob said. "In any case, we've found a suitable mate for you and we've set up a time for you to meet her tomorrow evening."

Isaac tried to explain. "But I-"

"No buts; it's time to take life seriously. If you're going to be baptized as Amish you must get yourself together." Jacob looked directly at his son. "Now this Sunday starts the next session of baptism meetings."

"But I'm not sure I'm ready for that."

"Of course you are," Jacob said, looking at his wife, Mary.

Isaac started, "But *Mudder* and *Daed*…"

"Tomorrow you will meet your soon to be wife," Mary said.

The two of them left the room without another word.

Chapter 6

It can't go on like this. I will have to do something.

Isaac knew that his parents wouldn't listen to him. He had to make a decision, and make it quick. Instead of meeting the girl his parents had chosen for him, Isaac sneaked out into town again and saw Sarah. This time he approached her as if his life depended on it.

"Why are you so nervous, Isaac?"

"Because I have something very important to say and it will not be easy," he explained.

"What is it?"

"My parents want me to meet and marry a girl of their choice."

"And what did you tell them?"

"I am here now instead of there, aren't I? I could not tell them anything because they wouldn't listen, but I am in love with you and I have been since the very first time we met."

"I have felt the exact same way," Sarah said, inching closer to him on the couch.

"Will you marry me, Sarah? I know we haven't known each other very long but I am peculiar enough to know that you are peculiar too. We believe in the same things and I would love to help you produce music one day. I know I'm not ready yet because I haven't gone to school but if you'll have patience with me, I'll learn fast."

"I don't know what to say," she said.

Isaac held her close. "Just say, yes."

A single tear ran down Sarah's cheek. "But what about your parents and the…?"

"Look, I don't know about all of that but I do know what I've been called to do." Isaac knelt down in front of Sarah. "I will be forced to leave in order to marry you, and also in order to pursue my vision. But I love the Amish so I don't know where this road will lead me."

Sarah asked, "You don't?"

"No, I don't. But if you'll promise to follow me, I'll never lead you astray. It may take me back to the Amish after I've finished school and it might not. Everything will be revealed in time. But would you be willing to go back if it turns out to be the right thing to do?"

"Yes, I will marry you and yes, I will go back to the Amish if and when it turns out to be the right thing to do." Sarah allowed Isaac to dry her tears with his hand. "You're a good and godly man, Isaac and I trust you."

"You're the best thing that ever happened to me, Sarah. Now I can let the music in my head and heart be free," he said.

Sarah smiled and put her head on Isaac's shoulder. And then they talked and dreamed of their wedding day as the music in their heads played on.

Epilogue

It had been three years since that evening.

It wasn't an easy decision to choose Sarah and music over the Amish life. But it had turned out to be the right one in the end. Sarah's parents had given Isaac their full support, especially when they realized that Sarah was in love with an Amish boy who shared their deeply instilled values and heritage.

Isaac's parents weren't too happy about Isaac's decision to learn music. Isaac told them that he loved them very much, but he couldn't stay Amish and learn music at the same time. His parents realized they couldn't stop him, and Isaac left them with a smile and a promise that he would come back one day.

Isaac went on to learn music and had taken to it naturally. Sarah and Isaac were now not only married, but also produced wonderful Christian music together. They appreciated the unique way God had chosen them to spread His word.

All was well.

THE END

Made in the USA
San Bernardino, CA
15 May 2016